The Hungry Thing Returns

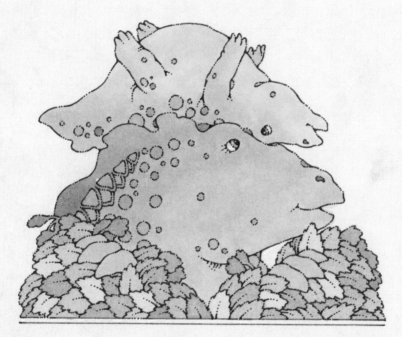

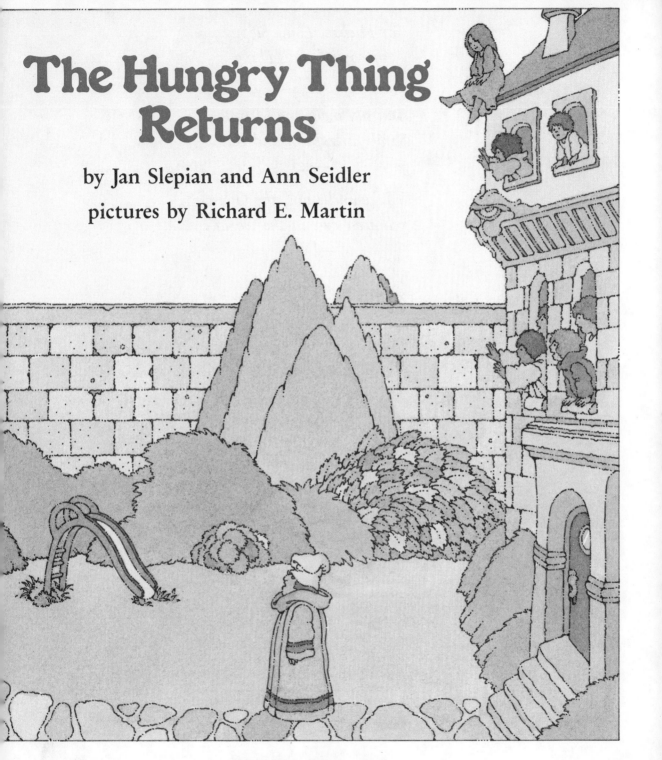

The Hungry Thing Returns

by Jan Slepian and Ann Seidler

pictures by Richard E. Martin

SCHOLASTIC INC.

New York Toronto London Auckland Sydney

For Michael Louis Slepian,
my own small Thing.
—J.S.

And my own small Things,
Sarah, Elizabeth, and Kate.
—A.S.

To Jake and Luke, the fattest,
yellowest cats in the world.
—D.M.

ISBN 0-590-42891-8

Text copyright © 1990 by Jan Slepian and Ann Seidler.
Illustrations copyright © 1990 by Scholastic Inc.
All rights reserved. Published by Scholastic Inc.

12 11 10 9 8 7 6 5 4 3   0 1 2 3 4 5/9

Printed in the U.S.A.

One day the Hungry Thing came into the school yard.
He carried a small Hungry Thing on his back.

Out of the school came the headmaster, the teachers,
and all the children. They gathered around the Hungry
Thing.

The Hungry Thing pointed to a sign around his neck.
It said **Feed Me**. The small Hungry Thing pointed to her
sign. It said **Me Too**.

"What would you like to eat?" asked the headmaster.

"Flamburgers," said the Hungry Thing.

"Flamburgers!" cried the school cook. "Dear me, let me
see. How do you eat them? What can they be?"

"Allow me," said a teacher. "Flamburgers I think,
are piles of spaghetti you eat in the sink."

"Not so," said the headmaster. "Flamburgers I know,
are chocolate-chip pickles that grow in the snow."

A child raised his hand. "I think," said the boy,
"flamburgers sound like...ramburgers...sound like...
hamburgers to me."

"Of course," said the headmaster. He told the cook to bring some.
The Hungry Thing and the small Thing ate them all up.

The Hungry Thing pointed to his sign that said **Feed Me**.

The small Thing pointed to her sign that said **Me Too**.

"What would you like to eat?" asked the headmaster.

"Bellyjeans," said the Hungry Thing.

"Bellyjeans!" cried the cook. "Dear me, let me see.

How do you eat them? What can they be?"

"But of course," said a teacher. "Bellyjeans I've read,
are square little pancakes you wear on your head."

"Bellyjeans are rare," said the headmaster. "They are handled with care when eaten by dragons in long underwear."

A child raised her hand. "I know," said the girl.
"Bellyjeans sound like...kellybeans...sound like...jelly beans to me."
"Of course," said the headmaster. He told the cook to bring some.

The Hungry Thing and the small Thing ate them all up.

The Hungry Thing rubbed his stomach. He pointed to his sign that said **Feed Me**. The small Thing pointed to her sign that said **Me Too**.

The teachers began to worry.

"I don't believe they'll ever leave."

"It's just not right, such appetite."

"I fear the worst. What if they burst?"

"Remember our manners," said the headmaster. "What would you like to eat?" he asked the visitors.

"Blownuts," said the Hungry Thing.

"Blownuts!" cried the cook. "Dear me, let me see. How do you eat them? What can they be?"

"I've heard," said a teacher, "that blownuts taste great.
They are round furry fishes that roll on your plate."

"That's right," said the headmaster. "Blownuts can float. With a wink and a smile, they'll jump into your boat."

Many hands went up.

A boy with glasses said, "It's easy. Blownuts sound like...shownuts...sound like...doughnuts to me."

The cook gave them some. The Hungry Thing and the small Thing ate them all up.

The small Thing began to squirm. She couldn't sit still. She whispered into her father's ear.

"Mathboom," the Hungry Thing told the headmaster.

"Mathboom!" cried the cook. "How do you eat it? What can it be?"

The headmaster didn't know. The teachers didn't know.

One girl went up to the Hungry Thing. She said, "Mathboom sounds like just one thing to me. Does your little girl need...the bathroom?"

The Hungry Thing nodded. He lowered his head, and the small Thing slid off. The girl took her to the bathroom.

When they returned, the small Thing would not climb
onto her father's back. She went down the slide instead.

The Hungry Thing stopped her. He placed her on his back once again.

He pointed to his sign that said **Feed Me**. But the small Thing hid her face.

"What would you like to eat?" asked the headmaster.

"Crackeroni and sneeze," the Hungry Thing answered.

"Crackeroni and sneeze!" said the cook. "Let me see. How do you eat it? What can it be?"

A teacher said, "Crackeroni and sneeze is a slippery dough. When you catch it and eat it, it makes your nose grow."

"It tastes like a roast," added the headmaster. "I prefer it on toast. It's especially good when you dine with a ghost."

All hands were raised. A boy with freckles said,
"Crackeroni and sneeze sounds like...snackeroni and
bees...sounds like...macaroni and cheese to me."

"Why of course," said the headmaster. The cook brought some.
The Hungry Thing ate it all. He wiped his mouth on
the headmaster's sleeve. He was ready to leave.

But where was the small Thing? She was playing on the slide again.

This time, when the Hungry Thing lifted her off, she began to cry. She would not stop. The Hungry Thing tried to comfort her.

"Oh, no! They were about to go! I do confess we're in a mess," said the headmaster.

The children tried to help. "What does she like best?" they asked the Hungry Thing.

"Harshfellows," he replied.

They brought her marshmallows. She didn't stop crying.

"Mice dream," said the Hungry Thing.

They gave her ice cream. She didn't stop crying.

"Gubble bum," said the Hungry Thing.

They offered her bubble gum. Nothing made her stop crying.

The Hungry Thing put his head on his claws. He did not know what to do.

The schoolchildren whispered to one another. Then one child whispered to the headmaster.

He said, "What a splendid idea," and set everyone to work.

Carefully, they lifted the slide and hung it around the neck of the Hungry Thing. The small Thing hugged it.

"For you to take home," they told her.

The Hungry Thing smiled. He turned his sign around. In big letters it said **Thank You**.

The small Thing was worn out. She was fast asleep with her head on the slide. The Hungry Thing turned her sign around. It said **Me Too**.